Black Angels

ALL AGES COLORING BOOK

BY: A.C. WASHINGTON

ILLUSTRATIONS BY:
ROXY HANA
ALBANY RIVILLO
SMRITI SARAOGI
JULIA MOOLEN

Black Angels

ALL AGES COLORING BOOK

Copyright © 2021 by A.C. Washington

No part of this book may be used or reproduced in any manner whatsoever without the prior written permission of the author.

ISBN: 9781737200109

Find more info at scruffypuppress.com

This Book Belongs To:

EVERY DAY iS
A BLESSiNG

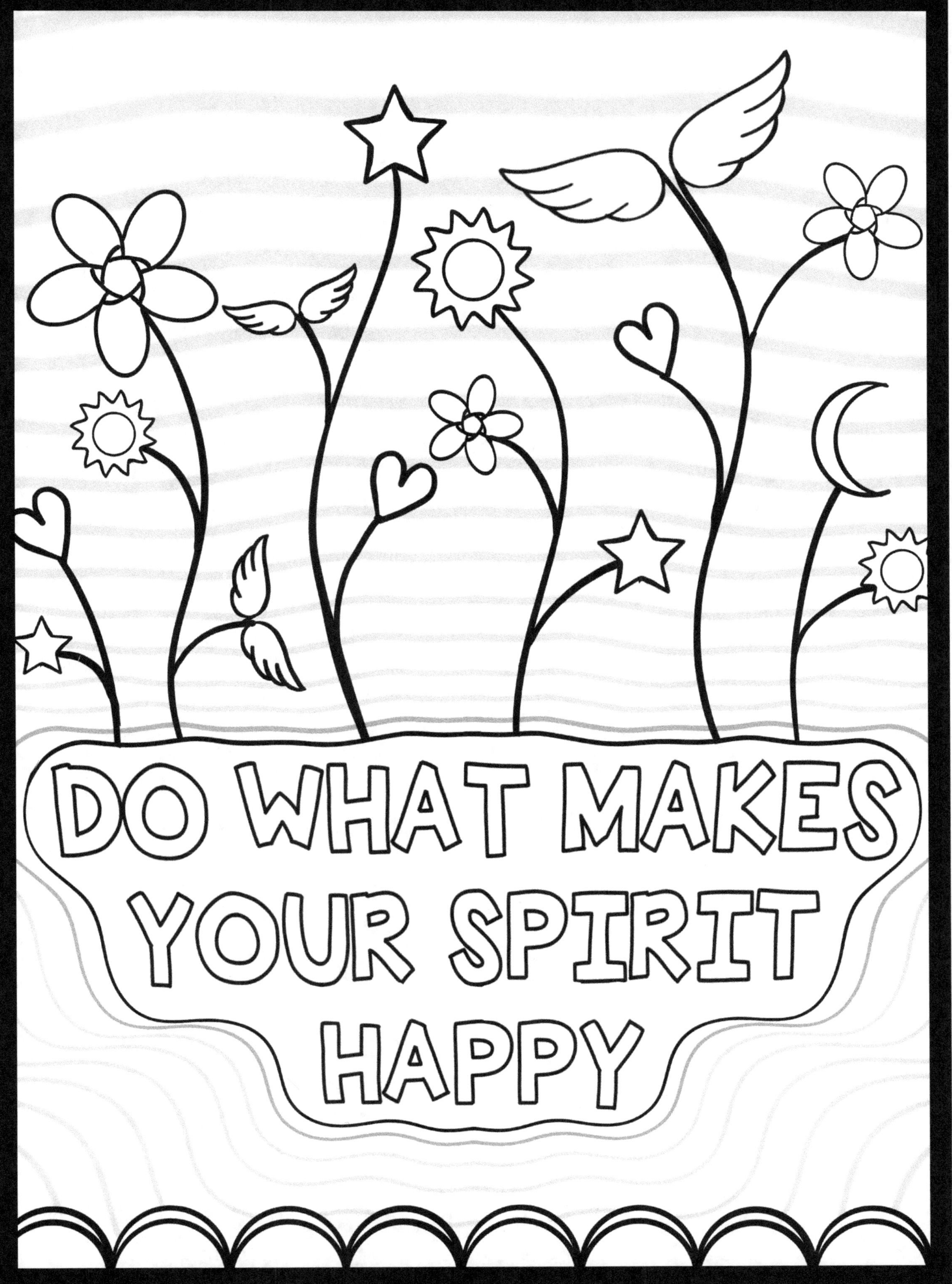

DO WHAT MAKES
YOUR SPIRIT
HAPPY

I AM AMAZING.
I AM LOVED.
I AM ENOUGH.

i BELiEVE THERE
iS GOOD
iN THE WORLD

ANGELS ARE
WATCHING
OVER ME

i BELIEVE iN MYSELF

Thank you for your purchase!

Find more books at
ScruffyPupPress.com.

If you enjoyed this coloring
experience, please leave a
review on Amazon!

Scruffy Pup Press